This book belongs to:

To Andrée

COMET THE FAIRY DOG
A RED FOX BOOK 978 0 099 43932 5 (from January 2007)
0 099 43932 8

First published in Great Britain in 2006 by Red Fox,
an imprint of Random House Children's Books
Originated by THE BODLEY HEAD

1 3 5 7 9 10 8 6 4 2

Red Fox Books are published by Random House Children's Books,
61-63 Uxbridge Road, London W5 5SA,
a division of The Random House Group Ltd,
in Australia by Random House Australia (Pty) Ltd,
20 Alfred Street, Milsons Point, Sydney, NSW 2061, Australia,
in New Zealand by Random House New Zealand Ltd,
18 Poland Road, Glenfield, Auckland 10, New Zealand,
and in South Africa by Random House (Pty) Ltd,
Isle of Houghton, Corner Boundary Road & Carse O'Gowrie,
Houghton 2198, South Africa

THE RANDOM HOUSE GROUP Limited Reg. No. 954009
www.kidsatrandomhouse.co.uk

A CIP catalogue record for this book is available from the British Library

Printed in China

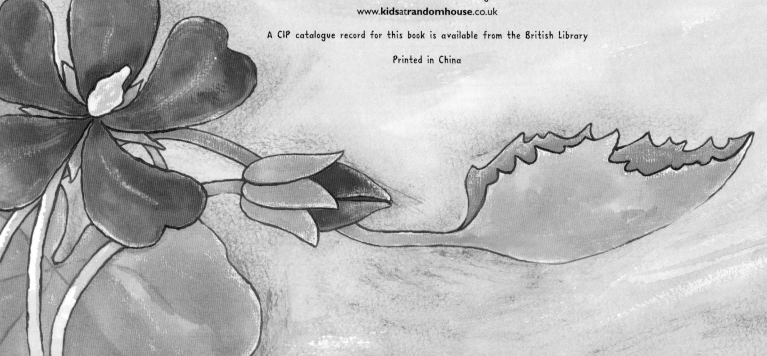

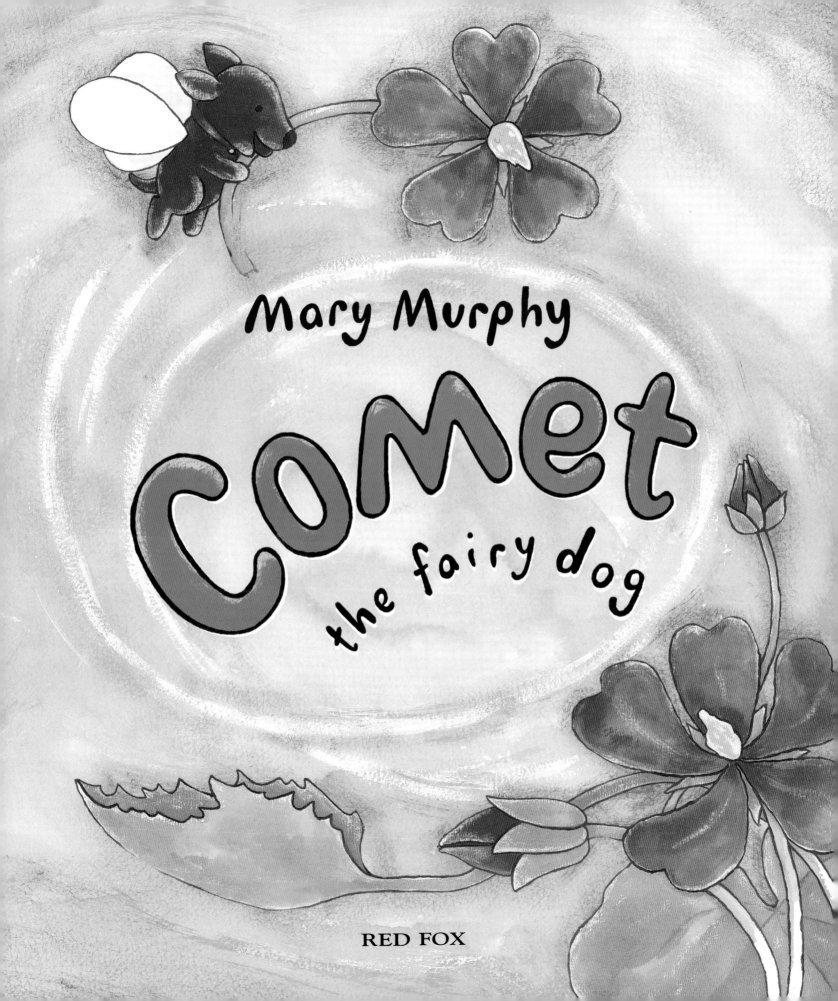

Mary Murphy

Comet
the fairy dog

RED FOX

This book
is about
me,
Comet
the fairy dog

and I hope you like it.

This is what I look like.
I am bigger than a bee,
and smaller than a mouse,
and I can fly.

Me – actual size.

The first thing I did
was get born. I was
a helpless baby.

Fairy dogs
have one puppy
at a time.

At last my eyes opened, and I
saw my mother's soft, kind face.

Fairy pups
open their eyes
at two weeks old.

I began to grow.
Soon I could walk.

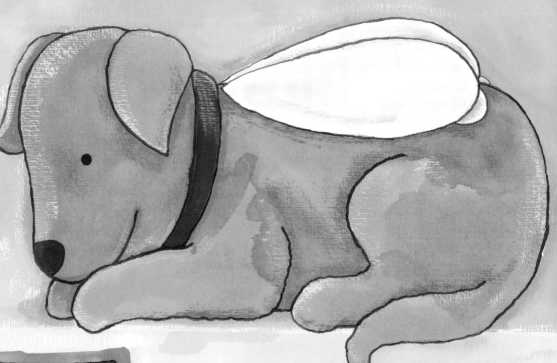

I spent all day
with my mother.

My mother flying me
around on her back.

Then I learned to fly.

Fairy pups
fly at three
months old.

I wanted

to

fly!

and

fly

I learned lots of other things too . . .

Baking

Sharing

Reading

Making light

Hiding

Fairy dogs shine when they move their wings at night.

Knowing friends

Knowing enemies

Drawing

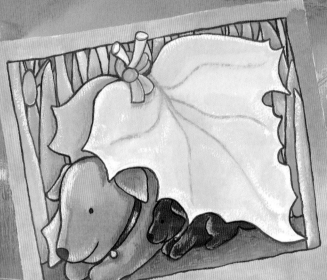
Camping

Finding my way

but flying was the best.

Our home was an old shoe, cosy and clean, under a blackberry bush. I loved it, but it would not be my home for ever. When I was one year old it was time to find a home of my own.

I said goodbye
to my mother.
"Good luck, Comet!"
she said.
Then I flew out into
the world.

I flew away from our shoe, over the blackberry bush, past the oak tree, to the stream at the end of the garden. There I saw a boat. "What a great home!" I said.

I cast off and sailed down the stream.

Faster and faster we went, until suddenly the boat tipped over.

Phew, it's a good thing I can fly!

"That boat wasn't a great home at all!" I said.
So I tried . . .

. . . an old nest with lovely views.

But it was too spiky and wobbly for a fairy dog.

. . . an empty rabbit burrow.

It was nice and cool, but too wet for me.

. . . a bird box.

It was happy and friendly, but too crowded for a fairy dog.

. . . a clean and cosy tree hollow.

It was too noisy for anyone except Owl.

"Somewhere in the garden is the perfect fairy dog home for me," I thought.

. . . Wicked Cat leaped out from the lavender bush,

slashing her claws at me.

Phew, it's a good thing I can fly!

I zipped off
in a flash.
Wicked Cat
chased me.

I flew faster.

Then it began to rain.

Disaster!

Now how was I going to escape from Wicked Cat?

Fairy dogs can't fly when their wings are wet.

"Quick! This way!"
squeaked a little voice.
"Wicked Cat hates thistles!"
It was a grey mouse, peeping out
from the thistle forest. I ran after her
into an upside-down flowerpot.

The flowerpot was cosy and clean.
The rain pattered on the roof like a friendly drummer.
I sat with my new friend, safe and dry.

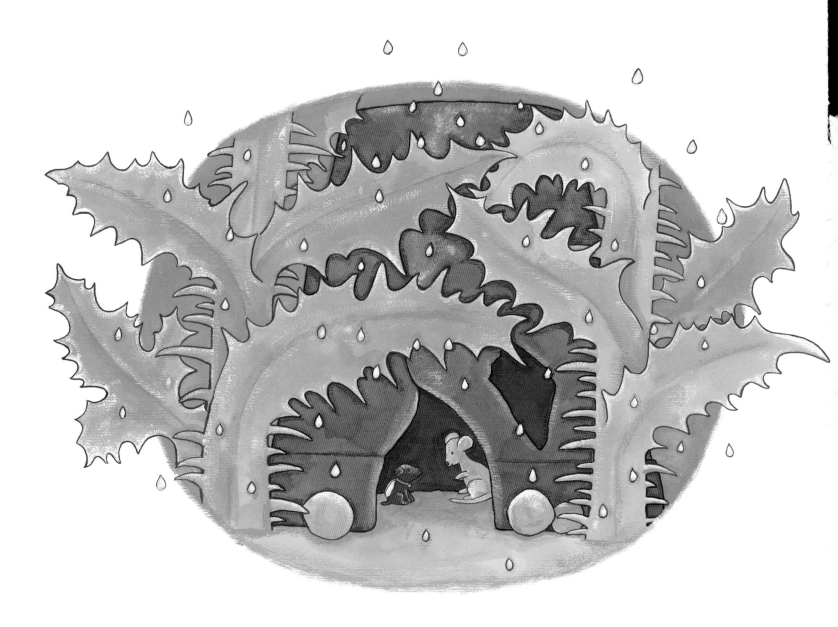

It felt like home.

And now it *is* home.
It is my fairy dog upside-down
flowerpot home. I live near lots of friends.
Do you know one thing fairy dogs love
about living near friends?

Visiting!

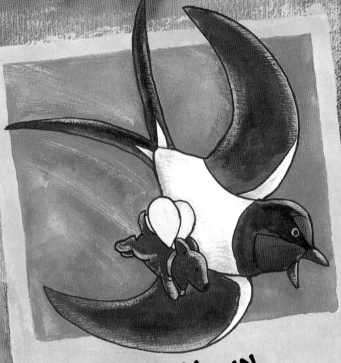

Swallow

Snail

Grace the house dog

Angel the baby rabbit

Owl

Grey Mouse

Sometimes I visit Mum in the old shoe,
under the blackberry bush.

Sometimes she visits me in my upside-down flowerpot
home, in the thistle forest, near the shed.
And sometimes . . .

Other books you might enjoy:

Cleopatra Silverwing
by Adria Meserve

A Chick Called Saturday
by Joyce Dunbar and Brita Granström

Who Will Sing My Puff-a-Bye?
by Charlotte Hudson and Mary McQuillan

Baby Bear's Christmas Kiss
by John Prater

A Pipkin of Pepper
by Helen Cooper

Where Did That Baby Come From?
by Debi Gliori